Disney
Winnie the Pooh

What Is That Rumbly In My Tummy?

Pooh woke up one morning with a delicious idea in his head.
"I think I'm in the mood for some honey pancakes," he thought.

So he got out everything he needed: eggs, milk, flour, and honey! He began to pour and mix the ingredients as he hummed a silly Pooh song:

Stir up the batter, yummy, yum, yum.
I can hardly wait for pancakes in my
tummy, tum, tum....

"I can almost taste them now,"
Pooh said, licking his lips and
rubbing his tummy. But then his
tummy made a strange sound.
  "RUMBLE-GRUMBLE," it said.

Pooh stopped what he was doing.

"Oh, dear," said Pooh. "Did you say something, tummy?"

"RUMBLE-GRUMBLE," his tummy replied.

"I don't understand—could you please repeat that?"

"RUMBLE-GRUMBLE!" said his tummy, even louder than before.

Pooh was puzzled. Clearly, his tummy was trying to tell him something, but he wasn't sure what.

"It was quite loud, so it must be important," he said. "I better find out."

"RUMBLE-GRUMBLE," his tummy seemed to agree.

"I suppose the pancakes will just have to wait," said Pooh, hurrying off to ask his friends' advice.

He first went to see Piglet who was busy cleaning his home.

"What is that rumbly in my tummy?" Pooh asked.

But Piglet had a problem of his own.

"I'd like to AH-CHOO help. But I AH-CHOO can't stop sneezing,"
Piglet explained. "It must be the dust tickling my nose. AH-CHOO-
CHOO-CHOO! Sorry, I can't help YOU-YOU-YOU!"

"Well, thank ah-choo, I mean *you*, anyway," said Pooh,
heading off in search of someone else who might know.
He found Tigger bouncing through the Wood.

"HIC-HIC-BOING!" said Tigger.

"Oh, Tigger," called Pooh. "I'm wondering if you can help me with a strange rumbly sound I have in my tummy...."

"Sorry, Pooh Ol' Pal. HIC-HIC-BOING. Can't stop to talk right now. I gulped down a glass of lemonade, and now my HIC-HIC-BOING insides are bouncin' as much as my HIC-HIC-BOING outsides!"

"I see," said Pooh. "Well, why don't you stop hiccupping?"
"I would if I could," answered Tigger. "HIC-HIC-BOING.
I've tried everything—even bouncing upside down."
"Like this?" asked Pooh.

"Exackatakly," called Tigger as he bounced away. "Good luck!"

Next, Pooh went to Eeyore's house. "Can you help me, Eeyore?" Pooh asked.

"Probably not, but I can try," replied Eeyore.

"Everyone I've asked so far has been making funny noises, and I have a strange sound of my own, you see. It's a loud rumbly in my tummy...."

Eeyore listened hard to Pooh's tummy.
"I don't hear anything," he said.
"Well, listen some more," pleaded Pooh.

"Nothin'," said Eeyore.

"Not a rumbly? Not a grumbly?" asked Pooh. "Maybe it was more of a bumbly or even a tumbly?"

"Nope," said Eeyore. Then he yawned a really big yawn. "YAHHH!"

"RUMBLE GRUMBLE!" said Pooh's tummy.
"There it is!" said Pooh excitedly. "Did you hear it?"
Eeyore yawned again. "Nope," he said. "I was yawning."

Owl was Pooh's last hope.
"If anyone knows what the rumbly in
my tummy means, it's Owl," he said.
But this time, not even Owl could help.

"Oh, bother," said Pooh. "Owl, won't you please wake up? This is terribly important!"

Owl's mouth was wide open.

"ZZZZZZ-WHISTLE-HEEEE," Owl snored. "ZZZZ-WHISTLE-WHOOO."

Pooh's tummy piped up again. "RUMBLE-GRUMBLE."
"I suppose I'll have to figure this out all by myself," said Pooh.
What Pooh needed was a little snack to help him think. He
remembered that his nearest honeypot was in his Thinking Spot.

Pooh was puzzled. Everyone's body was making a different funny sound—and each sound meant something else.

Piglet's nose sneezed when it was tickled by dust; Tigger's insides bounced when he hiccupped; Eeyore yawned when he was tired; and Owl made those funny snoring sounds when he slept with his mouth open.

Pooh was so busy thinking, he hardly realized he'd finished the entire
pot of honey.

"All gone, already?" Pooh said with a sigh as he licked his sticky paws.

Then he noticed that something else was gone—the rumbly in
his tummy!

"Hello in there," Pooh addressed his tummy. "You're awfully quiet
now! Would you please explain yourself?"

But Pooh's tummy wasn't talking.

"Let's see," Pooh said, scratching his head. "Those rumbly noises started right before breakfast."

BREAKFAST! Pooh had been so worried about his rumbly tummy, he'd completely forgotten to have his breakfast.

"That's it! Why was there a rumbly in my tummy? Because my tummy was telling me that I was hungry!" said Pooh, patting his tummy. "You should have said so in the first place!"

"I guess," Pooh announced, licking his sticky fingers, "my tummy loves honey just as much as I do!"

What Is My Body Trying to Tell Me?

Maybe you wake up in the morning, hungry as a Pooh Bear, with a rumbly in your tummy. Or sometimes just the smell of something yummy baking in the oven (like chocolate chip cookies) makes your stomach roar, as if to say, "Hurry up! Send some of those down here!"

Those strange gurgles and growls you may hear are really the sounds of the stomach walls squeezing together in an attempt to mix and digest food. Just one problem: there's no food there! Gases and digestive juices slosh around in your empty stomach, and before you know it, you have a whole symphony of strange sounds.

Your stomach is trying to tell you, "Your body needs fuel!" How does it know? Our brains contain a "hunger center," which, once necessary nutrients are lacking from the blood, tells the stomach to speak up.

Young children learn by playing, listening, observing, and describing. Here's a fun mix and match game to play with your child:

Match the sounds your body makes (Column A) to what it's trying to tell you (Column B).

COLUMN A	COLUMN B
Sneezing	"I'm hungry!"
Hiccupping	"Don't drink your chocolate milk so fast!"
Yawning	"Wow! I can't believe you ate the whole pizza!"
Tummy Growling	"Sweet dreams!"
Burping	"I'm tired...."
Snoring	"That dust tickles my nose!"